Acknowledgements

The author would like to thank all those who have helped in the completion of this book, in particular members of Writer Together – Bristol, Louise Boulton, Temi Garrick and Bethan Thomas.

First published in Great Britain in 2022 by Magnetical

A catalogue record for this book is available from the British Library

Designed by James Pople
Edited by Craig Simpson
Proofread by Joanna Peios

ISBN: 978 1 9160646 5 2

Printed and bound in the United Kingdom by IngramSpark

THE CARPENTER AND THE GOAT HERDER

MERLIN GOLDMAN

MAGNETICAL

CHAPTER ONE

A FEW DROPS OF RAIN FELL ON THE DONKEY'S BACK, RUNNING IN RIVULETS AROUND HIS HAUNCHES. HE SHIVERED. KIP MUEMBA SMILED AS HE HANDED THE WOMAN THE TEAK BOWL. SHE'D HAGGLED HARD AND GOTTEN A GOOD PRICE FROM HIM. BUT IT HAD BEEN A DECENT ENOUGH DAY: HE'D SOLD TWO DINING CHAIRS AND SEVERAL CUPS AND BOWLS.

CHAPTER ONE

As Kip loaded his cart, the rain intensified. Most of the other stallholders had packed up and left. The remaining few hurried away. The droplets grew heavy, exploding on impact with the dry ground. The donkey's ears shook others away.

The cart bobbled over the softening track making the ruby beads on Kip's thick wrist jostle for position. Their colour deepened under the rolling black clouds. The medicine woman had said everything would be okay. Pushing through the heavy scarlet curtains into her tent on the edge of the market, it had been cool and filled with the scent of black coconut. Squat candles had lit the dark interior.

Sitting cross-legged on a cushion, her grey dreadlocks knotted on top of her head, she asked, 'What is troubling you?'

Kip bowed his head. 'It's my wife. She's in a lot of pain.'

She motioned for him to sit down.

Settling onto an oval cushion, he added, 'I'm worried about her. And the child she carries.'

'Do you believe in magic?'

'If it keeps them safe.'

The medicine woman tutted. 'You must have faith. If you have no faith, then there is nothing I can do.'

Kip wrung his hands. 'I want everything to be okay. Just tell me what to do?'

The woman studied him. 'I can see you are a good man. A truthful man. Hold out your hand.' Kip leant forward and stretched out his right arm, pulling back the sleeve of his cream shirt.

The woman rolled the bracelet over his wrist. 'Keep this on you at all times. It will bring you good fortune.'

Kip paid the woman and returned home. His wife asked him where it had come from, and he lied. She didn't believe in witchcraft.

When his wife went into labour, their neighbour, Rudi, did what she could. The doctor had been taken by the warlord on his last raid. Others tried to help but she died. His daughter took three breaths then followed. His wife had been right; magic was for fools.

Kip flicked the reins to keep the donkey moving. Its muscles flexed beneath its grey-white rump with each stride. Potholes became black mirrors. Kip drove them on faster as sheets of mud slid down the inside bank. The donkey's legs buckled when a wheel sunk into the ground, throwing Kip forward, the bracelet snagging on the cart's frame. Its string snapped. The beads scattered, clattering over the cart, most swept over the edge.

Mud flowed over Kip's sandals as he checked the donkey was unharmed. He grabbed the few beads left on the cart. He peered about the ground, diving here and there to retrieve those he spotted before they sunk into the silt and were washed away.

Kip knelt down, plunging his hands into the sludge, feeling for beads. Clenching his hands into fists, liquid escaped between his fingers. Any bead left in his palm was pushed into his top pocket. Kip saved a few more but most were lost.

Revealing his palms to the sky, he let the rain wash them clean. He wept for the first time since he'd lost his family. Gathering the few beads he'd rescued, he threw out his arm, hurling the beads like seeds onto a field.

Leaning both arms on the cart, and dropping his head between them, he let the rain lash his back. He heard a cry. He lifted his head and tried to dampen the rain's drumbeat. He heard the cry again and pushed himself off the cart. He tried to decipher it. Someone was calling for help. It was close, so it must be from one of the nearby fields. Kip peered searchingly through the rain and saw a small figure in white amongst a herd of animals.

Leaping over the roadside ditch and into the field, he jogged towards her. The animals were goats. They bleated loudly as he approached what he realised was a young girl, her hands covering her face as she cried.

Kip stood over her. 'What's wrong?'

She spread her fingers and inspected him with her large, teal blue eyes.

'Why are you upset, little girl?'

She dropped one hand to her side and pointed with the other. 'My goat is stuck,' she whimpered, 'and the others won't go home without her.'

The goat was wedged in a hedge make from spiky Pao piku bushes. Kip took his knife from his belt and approached the beast. It pulled harder at the bush, drawing blood and ringing the bell hanging from its neck. The girl followed Kip, her arms flapping at her sides. 'What are you going to do?'

'Don't worry,' he said, straddling the goat to hold it still.

'Don't hurt her!'

Kip sliced the prickly branches clinging to its leather collar. The goat bleated and tried to wriggle free. Kip squeezed his legs tighter as thorns scratched his skin. The bell rattled. He cut away the last branch and stepped back. It jumped, turned sharply and galloped to the herd.

'Danki,' said the girl.

Thunder rumbled.

'You should go home.'

Lightning flashed.

'I'm not afraid.'

'Well, I am.' Kip sheathed his knife and walked back towards the road. 'And I don't want to be struck here.'

She tasted the rain then frowned. 'Do you miss them?'

Kip stopped. 'Who?'

The girl said nothing, tilting her head as she watched Kip's shoulders slump.

'Every day. I think about what they were and what they might have been.' He turned to face her. 'How do you know?'

'Your tears mixed with the rain.' She clasped her arms around her tiny body. 'I felt them through you.'

Thunder rolled across the heavens. Branched lightning, like a tree's roots, briefly lit her face. Her body glowed white.

'I've no time for magic. Leave me be.'

Kip trudged back to his cart. He tightened the ropes holding down the tarpaulin and climbed back up. His clothes felt like weights pulling him down.

'Right, donkey, let's go.' He flicked the reins, making raindrops. The donkey dragged them out of the sticky mud. They trundled away. He glanced back at the field, but it was empty.

CHAPTER TWO

KIP AND THE DONKEY MADE
SLOW PROGRESS ALONG
THE SLIPPERY TRACK TO
THE VILLAGE. THE RAIN WAS
UNRELENTING. IT GREW DARKER.
THE DONKEY NEEDED CONTINUAL
ENCOURAGEMENT TO DRAG
THEM HOME. KIP FELL ASLEEP
SEVERAL TIMES, ONLY TO BE
SHAKEN AWAKE BY THUNDER,
AND TO FIND THEM MOTIONLESS.

CHAPTER TWO

Turning the final corner, the lush top of the ancient gaboon tree was lit up by a lightning flash. It was said it was the reason the village was built here. There were few of its kind left.

The cart jolted and Kip woke with the trunk a few metres dead ahead. Pulling sharply on the left rein, they veered away. A back wheel ran over a thick root, jolting him out of his seat, returning with a bump.

Kip guided them to the barn attached to his house. He unhooked the donkey and it trotted inside. It nibbled on some crisp straw. He went indoors – he'd unpack the cart in the morning.

The fire's embers hissed as raindrops fell through the chimney. Each thunderclap shook the building.

'Close,' he muttered to himself as he peeled off his clothes.

Reanimating the fire with fresh wood, he wrapped himself in a wool blanket the colour of a sweet berry, dropped into his rocking chair, and fell asleep.

Kip dreamt of a green fire engulfing the village. It roared as it burnt their homes to the ground. Those who escaped were caught by a giant hand and thrown back.

Cool sunlight filled the room. Outside, someone called his name. Banging on his front door yanked him from sleep. Kip stood. The blanket slipped to the floor. 'I'm coming.' Reaching down, he pulled it back up around him and shuffled to the door.

Dayo, the son of Rudi and Axel, stood outside. The boy's clothes were muddy and a patch of blood had dried on his forehead.

'We need your help,' he blubbered. 'Father asks you to bring your axe.'

'What...?' Kip began, but the boy had run off. The sun was already burning off the remains of the previous night's storm.

He dressed, tying a rust-coloured handkerchief around his neck, and fetched an axe from his workshop. Maybe they'd trapped a wild dog in the chicken pens.

Kip jogged into the centre of town, past the well and towards the crowd of villagers. It seemed everyone was there. They gesticulated and shouted. Kip stopped, aghast: the gaboon tree had fallen, crushing Rudi and Axel's house. He pushed through the throng, coming face-to-face with the base of the tree and its nest of roots. Several were torn or twisted, their inner white flesh wet. Worms wriggled in the clinging soil. Dayo held his father's hand and pointed at Kip.

An elder gripped Kip's shoulder. 'Thank god you've come.'

'What happened?'

CHAPTER TWO

'Didn't you hear it? The tree fell in the lightning storm. Rudi is trapped inside her house.'

Axel rushed to Kip, shaking his clasped hands. 'Please, Kip, we don't know what to do.'

Some of the villagers protested. Kip hadn't spoken properly to most of them for years. Each had offered platitudes following the tragedy. But what practical use are kind words, he thought. But he listened. Each had a different idea as to how to free Rudi.

Kip examined the tree. It had fallen through the middle of the house, splitting in two. The roof and two of the walls leant against it. The tree wasn't flat but balanced at its midpoint by the brass headboard of Rudi and Axel's bed. The treetop hovered a metre over the ground, branches bent. The bark was soft but inside it was as hard as rock.

Zuberi, the barber, made towards Kip, leading a small group. He rubbed his bald head. 'Kip will agree with me: we should pull the tree from its roots.'

'No, no,' said Hagos, the butcher, pushing forward. 'We need to roll it.'

'Rubbish, we should lift the tree with pulleys,' said Sekai, the baker, motioning with his hands in front of his pot belly.

Kip ran his hand along the bark. A lightning bolt had torn through it, burning its way from the crown to the base.

Rudi cried out.

'Mummy,' whimpered Dayo, gripping Axel's hand. Even conflicted, the villagers knew they had to decide quickly.

Kip swung the blade into the tree trunk, embedding it. They all turned towards him. 'We have nothing to attach pulleys to, so we cannot lift it. If we roll it, a wall will crush Rudi. If we pull it, it may slide sideways, hurting Rudi even more.'

Kip tapped the axe handle. 'But if we cut it here, the weight of the tree will flip up and we can pull out the bed before Rudi is crushed.'

Zuberi, Hagos and Serkai filled their lungs and voiced their objections until Axel silenced them. 'Tell us what to do?'

Kip instructed the villagers to remove the thinnest branches from the crown. Children crawled under the collapsed house and tied ropes to the legs at the end of the bed. Kip swung at the tree, slicing through the dry bark, sending small chips spinning through the air.

The elders organised fresh water and food to be brought. Kip swung from his left then his right until he'd created a deep 'V' in the caramel wood. Each swing drove deeper. The tree creaked and sweat puddled on his face.

Approaching the tree's heart, the wood grew denser. Each swing cut less deep than the last. Kip stopped to drink. Rudi moaned, calling for Axel. Each small shift of the tree pushed and twisted a branch into her side. The brass bed frame creaked, and the remaining structure of the house sank a little further.

Kip swung until he reached the core of the trunk. But the axe refused to cut any further. He examined the blade, but it was still sharp.

CHAPTER TWO

Axel stood by Kip's shoulder. 'What's wrong? Why have you stopped?'

'It will not cut. The mahogany is hard.'

Part of the roof crashed to the ground. A woman screamed.

'Please,' implored Axel, his hands clasped.

Kip took off his neckerchief. It was soaked with sweat, but he wiped his face anyway. He squeezed it dry then examined the black core of the tree trunk, which felt like a bottomless well he could fall into and never return. He ran the wet cloth along the blade's edge, making it glisten. In its reflection he thought he saw the goat herder, but when he turned there was no one there. He swallowed a cup of water, then returned to the tree.

Taking off his sandals, he set his feet wide apart, letting the smooth soil slip between his toes. He stared into the tree's black heart, dangling the axe head by his ankle. He swung it up and over his head and drove it down into the dark interior. He swung again. A chunk of wood like coal flew out. He swung again and again, cutting deeper, scattering black chips to the ground.

Rudi whined and Dayo tore himself from Axel's grip, running towards his mother. Kip paused. 'Get ready. I'm nearly through.'

Half a dozen villagers pulled the ropes taut. Children climbed inside the treetop and gripped branches. Axel pulled Dayo away, holding him against himself.

As Kip swung the axe towards the other side, the tool seemed weightless. He felt possessed of superhuman strength. The trunk creaked and the top half began moving upwards, bending the sliver of wood connecting the halves. Kip breathed in and swung again. The blade cleaved clean through. The tree groaned, the top crashing to the ground, shaking the leaves. Some of the children fell from the canopy. Rudi screamed.

'Pull!' shouted Kip.

Villagers pulled on the ropes, dragging the bed out. The end of the frame was now visible along with Rudi's feet. They pulled once more, but the bed was stuck. Again, they tried. The remnants of the roof slid towards Rudi. She held both hands to her stomach.

'It's stuck,' shouted Axel, pointing to Rudi, her back writhing against the frame.

Kip and Axel ran underneath and pulled Rudi's legs. The branch stuck in her side slid out, making her cry in agony. They carried her from the rubble as the remaining wall collapsed, followed by the roof.

The elders organised a party that evening. A mountainous fire was built, goats roasted and jerepigo wine drunk from bamboo cups. Young children threw the gaboon tree's branches onto the fire and jumped back with each pop as the sap boiled. Older children roasted guinea pigs skewered on arrows at the fire's edge. Blood-orange flames pulsed upwards in swathes. The air grew thick with smoke and a pungent, earthy aroma. Hagos beat a rhythm on his djembe as Serkai shook his gourd caxixi.

CHAPTER TWO

Kip crouched, staring into the fire. Someone approached and stood by him. 'My wife wants me to tell you how grateful she is,' said Axel.

Kip held his gaze. 'Will she be okay?'

'She should recover. With the doctor gone, she's been telling us how to treat her.'

Kip laughed. 'She sounds like she's going to be okay.'

'The elders want to give you something.'

Kip stood up, replying, 'I don't need anything,' and walked away.

At the tree, he traced the path of the lightning with his fingers. He dipped them into the jagged wound. It was curiously smooth and warm. And it had a *pulse*. He jerked his hand out.

Checking he was alone, he knelt and slid both hands into the scar. He felt the pulse again. It traversed up his arms and into his chest as if it were alive.

'What are you doing?' said Oba, the oldest elder.

'I will have this wood as my gift.'

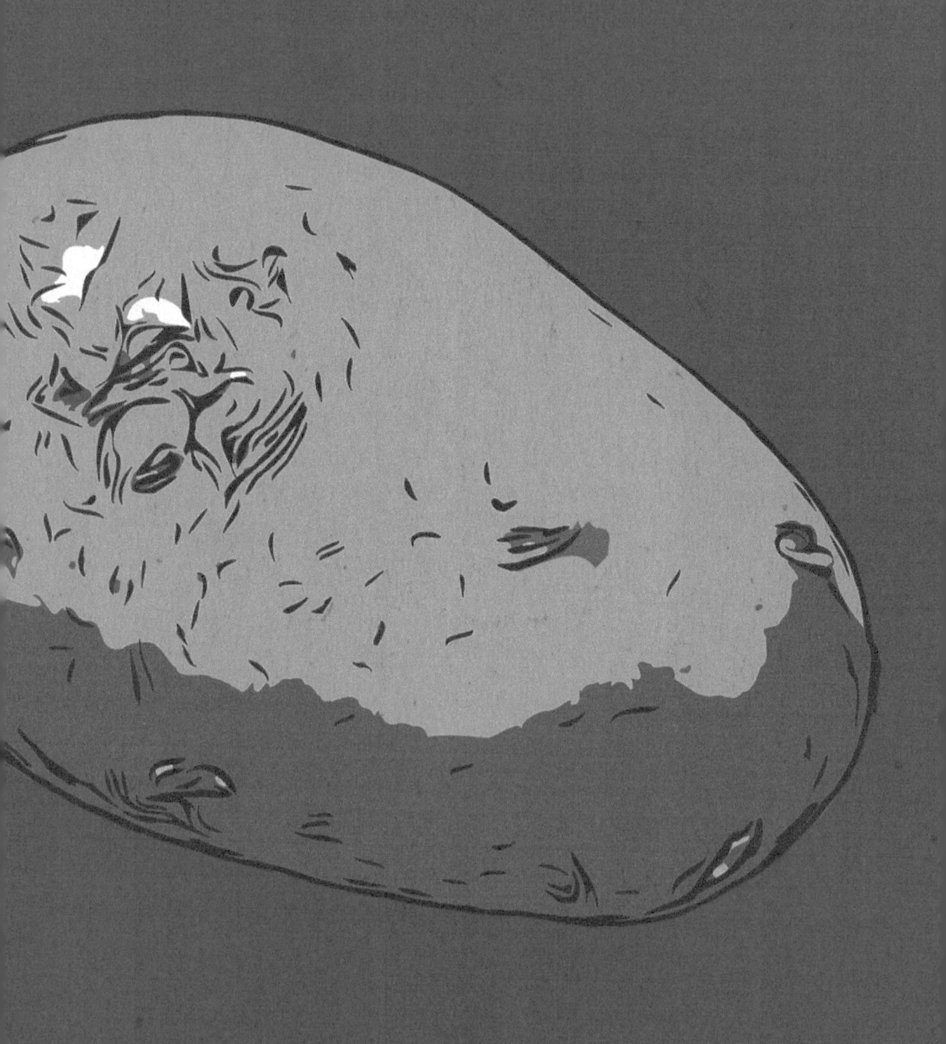

CHAPTER THREE

KIP WOKE EARLY. HE FED THE DONKEY AND ATE BREAKFAST. HE STRAPPED HIS TOOLKIT AROUND HIS WAIST THEN PUT A LEATHER AND METAL HARNESS OVER THE DONKEY. IT FOLLOWED HIM THROUGH THE VILLAGE, TRANQUIL AT THAT HOUR APART FROM A FEW DOGS FIGHTING OVER SCRAPS. A WISP OF SMOKE ROSE FROM THE FIRE'S EMBERS.

CHAPTER THREE

At the tree, Kip tied the donkey to the corner of the bed frame, cut through the roots and tidied the base until it was a clean disc. He hammered iron pegs around its circumference, blood-red sap seeping from each puncture. Positioning the donkey with its back to the trunk, he clipped the chains attached to its harness to the pegs.

Kip took hold of the donkey's reins. 'Okay, bra, time to pull.' The donkey stood its ground. Kip tugged again but the donkey remained impassive.

He stepped backwards, letting go of the reins. 'So, it's like that, is it?' The donkey turned away.

Kip pulled a sweet potato from a bag and held it out. The donkey stretched its neck, sniffing the air. It turned its head towards the potato. Kip stepped backwards and the donkey followed, eyes fixed on the dark orange treat.

'This is for you if you help me.'

The donkey stopped, the chains tight, and turned sideways. *Why do you have to be so difficult?* Kip waved the potato towards it. The donkey snapped back and bit off the top of the vegetable. 'Careful!' said Kip, 'You'll have my fingers.'

The donkey chewed on the morsel as Kip pulled it by the reins, holding the potato just out of reach. 'Now, pull.'

The donkey stepped forward and the trunk shifted. 'That's it.' The donkey pulled again, and the trunk jolted forward. 'Come on, my old friend.' The donkey hesitated. 'You're the strongest donkey in Africa.'

He threw the remains of the potato in front of the donkey. Standing beside it, he rested a hand on its flank. 'Let's go.'

The donkey tilted his head down and started to walk forwards. 'That's it!' shouted Kip. The harness rattled. The trunk crunched over the remnants of the house.

Once they cleared the debris, it was a smooth journey across the scorched, dusty earth. As long as Kip provided more sweet potatoes, the donkey kept moving.

Kip led them through the village. At the barn, he removed the harness and poured cool water over the donkey's back. 'Well done, bra,' he declared, tipping out the final sweet potato from his bag.

Kip used a hoist to raise the trunk onto a pair of V-shaped plinths. He removed the pegs and wiped off the dried sap. Now that he had it, he wondered what he would make with it. He'd never worked with mahogany of such deep colour. Well, if he didn't start, it'd just sit there.

Kip prised off the bark. It snapped off in large chunks and slivers. The donkey paced in its stable, occasionally leaning over the partition to watch.

First sawing off a section at both ends, leaving a tapered piece of about six feet long and two feet thick, he planed the trunk until it was the same width throughout. He still didn't know what to make, perhaps a table, or a few chairs? He picked up a chisel. I'll remove some of the outer wood and see where it leads, he thought. The outer layers of soft wood came away easily. He felt guided and continued without being aware of villagers who stopped to watch before moving on. It didn't seem to matter what he was making but he couldn't stop. He moved to finer tools.

Kip worked through the day, never stopping. His arms and back ached but he kept going. The wood was strong, but he cut through it. Wood shavings piled up around his feet. The donkey scuffed the ground. The more Kip removed, the more he felt someone was there with them.

Zuberi stopped by and gave Kip news that Rudi was healing slowly and that the elders had organised a group of villagers to rebuild their house. His concentration broken, Kip covered the trunk with the donkey's red blanket and had dinner. He returned and worked through the night under a single bulb, tickled by moths.

As the air cooled, the wood remained warm. He used smaller chisels and rasps for the finer features, carving shadows into the morning until the figure of a woman emerged.

CHAPTER FOUR

KIP WOKE TO BANGING. IT WAS HIS FRONT DOOR. 'CARPENTER. COME OUT.' A VOLLEY OF GUNFIRE WAS FOLLOWED BY SCREAMS SOMEWHERE ELSE IN THE VILLAGE. THE WARLORD HAD RETURNED.

CHAPTER FOUR

Kip dressed then opened the door. Two soldiers in loose green uniforms stood outside. They were no more than fourteen. The oldest carried a rifle over his shoulder. He nudged the other, who directed Kip to the barn.

Kip's tools had been thrown to the ground and two unarmed soldiers threw his furniture into a pile.

'Hey!' shouted Kip, 'What are you doing?' He knew exactly, of course. They'd been expecting a visit for some time from the warlord's child army. Kip grabbed a chair and tried to take it back in but was knocked to the floor.

'What is going on here?' said a deep voice from above. Kip turned his head – it was Mzungu, the warlord. The big man stood, legs apart, dressed in camouflage battle fatigues, and wearing dark sunglasses.

'It's the carpenter, sir,' said one boy soldier. 'He's causing trouble.'

The village hadn't seen Mzungu for months and hoped he might not come back. He circled Kip's woodwork as Kip got to his feet. Mzungu usually took everything he could find, including children as soldiers, or women for his harem; anything to fuel his campaign of terror and accumulation of power.

'How is our doctor?' said Kip.

'She's good, good. Took a little while to break her in, but she's found her place now,' said Mzungu. He stopped at the covered trunk. 'What is this?'

'Nothing,' said Kip. 'It's not furniture, no good to you.'

The warlord touched the red blanket. The donkey shot

out of the barn, knocking his arm and the two soldiers to the ground.

'Shoot it,' said Mzungu.

The soldier boy fumbled the rifle as he tried to lift it to his shoulder. Mzungu snatched it from him and took aim. Kip jumped in front of him, moving side to side as Mzungu tried to get a line of sight.

'No, please, without it, I cannot get to the market to sell my furniture. Without it, I cannot fetch more wood.' He knew deep down that arguing would not work, but what else could he do?

Mzungu shifted his aim to Kip's head. He let out a large belly laugh, lowering the gun. 'A donkey! You'd take a bullet for a stupid donkey. You are a fool.'

Mzungu threw the gun back to the boy soldier. 'We'll take what you made at the market instead. As well as this furniture. It will look good in my bedroom.'

'Why do you do this?' said Kip as he was dragged back into his house.

A jeep pulled up and a soldier opened the door for Mzungu. He put one foot on the sill then turned to Kip. 'Because two men cannot laugh at the same time.'

The furniture was loaded onto a truck. Kip handed over what little money he'd made, emptying his cash box kept on the mantelpiece. More children were taken that day, but the carved gaboon trunk remained untouched.

Kip searched for his donkey throughout the village. Spilled grain sacks littered the east side and throughout, the crying of parents. 'They took five children,' said one of the elders, trying to attract his attention.

'It's not my concern,' said Kip. 'I'm looking for my donkey, have you seen him?'

'I thought you hated that donkey.'

'Often,' said Kip. 'But I need it.'

'We need to stop Mzungu. Soon we will have no children left.'

'What can I do?' said Kip.

After several hours, Kip returned home. It was nearly dark. The donkey was back in its stable, asleep. Kip shook his head and went indoors. He rocked in his chair, staring out of the window at the half moon holding the village in its silent grip.

CHAPTER FIVE

VISITING THE WELL, RUDI WAS THERE, WINCING WITH EACH PULL OF THE BUCKET. 'LET ME DO THAT,' KIP SAID, STRIDING OVER.

'NO!' SHE RESPONDED, SHRUGGING HIM AWAY. 'YOU'VE DONE ENOUGH FOR ME, AND THIS WAS DAYO'S TASK. I NEED TO DO IT.'

CHAPTER FIVE

Kip watched her fill two white plastic containers. A spot of blood formed on the side of her dress.

'Rumours are, you're working on something for yourself?'

'A small piece, nothing of value.'

'Most unlike you,' said a smiling Rudi. She lifted the ropes and walked homewards.

'I'm sorry about your son,' Kip called out, unsure if she'd heard him. The water sloshed out of the containers as they bumped against Rudi's knees. The donkey snorted. 'I'd like to see you do any better,' he muttered.

Kip lowered the bucket into the well. It took nearly the full length of the rope to reach the water these days. The donkey slurped on a puddle. When his containers were filled and attached to the donkey's harness, he topped-up his leather water bottle. He spotted a leak. 'Might be time for a new one. I wonder whether donkey leather might work.' He patted the donkey's rump. 'Let's go.'

Kip switched his attention to a table. He'd intended to sell it at market, but it would do as a dining table for Axel and Rudi. He carved a moon moth into its centre. They were staying with an elder while their house was rebuilt.

'How much do we owe you?' said Axel, helping Kip take it off the cart.

'Nothing. It's my contribution. Even if your wife is a bit of a busybody. How is she?'

'She will not stay still. The stitches in her side keep breaking.' Axel shook his head. 'She doesn't think we will ever see Dayo again if the warlord remains alive. I believe it too.'

Rudi appeared at the window.

Kip manoeuvred Axel so that the cart was between them and the house. 'What if we hire an assassin?'

'That's madness,' said Axel. 'What if they fail and the warlord finds out? He might kill us all. Or Dayo.'

'If we do nothing, you'll never see him again anyway.'

'What do the elders say?'

'I've not spoken to them. What good are they?'

Axel grabbed Kip's arms. 'Speak to them, Kip, please, before you do anything foolhardy.'

Kip shook himself loose. 'Let's take the table inside.'

When Kip climbed back onto the cart to leave, Axel stood by his feet. He checked quickly over his shoulder that his wife had gone back inside. 'Please, Kip, get their permission.'

Kip knelt on the woven mat in front of the three elders. They sat cross-legged on a softly furnished podium. The opaque tent was lit by soft light from oil-filled lamps. It was round and served many purposes: meeting place, court and wedding venue.

The elders listened to his plan. When he'd finished, Kip was asked to step outside. He thought of the goat herder, wondering what she'd think of his plan to hire an assassin. Would she approve? Why did he care what she thought?

CHAPTER FIVE

Kip was called back inside.

'This is a good idea,' said the first elder, slapping her hands on her wide thighs. 'We cannot go on having our food and children taken.'

The second shook her head. 'It's too dangerous. Mzungu will find out and do us more harm. I vote against.' She folded her arms and they both turned to their senior elder.

Kip studied her face, hoping for a sign. She shifted in her seat, tilting her head from side to side. Kip opened his arms, 'We must do something. They've stolen from me. From all of us. Enough is enough.'

'How much will it cost?' she asked.

'I do not know,' said Kip. 'Maybe one thousand.'

'At least a thousand,' said the second elder.

The first elder turned to the others. 'We will never get our children back unless we do something.'

'It's far too dangerous,' said the second. 'The village still stands. At some point, Mzungu will be killed in battle and our children returned to us. I still say "No".'

'I'm sorry, Kip,' said the senior elder, 'I'm against the idea. That's two to one against. Why don't you tell us about the new piece you've been working—' But Kip didn't hear the rest, as he'd already left their tent.

Inside the barn, he fell to his knees and began scraping away at the soil in the corner of the stable. A wooden box emerged. He pulled it out and wiped the top clean of the brown silt. His father had made the box for his mother. Inside was her wedding necklace. He let it twirl in the dying light, so it caught the three green emeralds encircling the gold pendant, a ruby at its centre. This was a fair sacrifice to return the village to how it had once been.

At the next market, Kip set up his stall as usual, although he had little furniture left to sell; mostly smaller items, bowls, spoons and cutting boards.

'We heard what happened,' said Kamaria, the stallholder next to him. She sold woven blankets and rugs. 'He killed my cousin when he refused to hand over his daughter.' She leant towards him. 'Mzungu slit his neck like a goat.'

Kip tapped his chest pocket. 'Would you watch my stall; I have to visit someone?'

She waved him away, fanning herself in the oppressive heat.

Kip hurried through the narrow back streets. The sun cut sharp lines into the walls and dogs slid by, scenting the ground. He reached the old shebeen he'd heard about and entered.

He bought a honey beer and sat at the bar. The mirror's black edges threatened to meet in the middle. Two men sat in one corner beneath coalescing clouds of smoke below the urine-coloured ceiling. The barman leant backwards, swigging from a bottle of beer. Kip considered the situation. He could leave now and life would return to normal. He had no children and could remake his goods. He could live a safe life.

Kip grabbed his glass and approached the table. One of the men rose and left, eyeballing Kip as he brushed past him.

CHAPTER FIVE

Kip sat down. 'I see you have a sweet tooth,' said the man. Smoke escaped through his teeth, drifting in front of his dark eyes, partially hidden by a brown Kakadu hat, pulled low over his brow.

'I wish to hire you.'

'To do what? Scare the crows from your fields?' He swallowed a mouthful of whisky through his teeth. He rolled the bevelled glass between his thumb and forefinger.

'I want you to kill Mzungu.'

The man slammed the glass onto the table. He grabbed his smouldering black cigar from the battered tin ashtray and leant back chuckling, then roared with laughter.

Kip checked the bar – it was empty. Even the barman had gone. The man leant forward; his features stilled. 'This is not a game, villager. Mzungu has an army.'

'Of boys,' said Kip, drinking steadily. 'Surely they don't frighten you?'

'I am not scared of anyone,' he snapped, swinging one arm in a circle. 'But he is a valuable target. Many others would wish him gone.'

'So go to them,' said Kip, standing up.

'Wait, wait,' said the man, patting him down. 'What do you have?'

Kip slid a roll of notes across the table. Several villagers had contributed. He hoped it would be enough. The assassin flicked the edges. 'Enough to cut his hair but not his neck.'

Kip pulled the necklace from his pocket and held it up. 'This will be enough.'

The assassin watched the pendant rotate. 'I will do it.' He grabbed for the necklace, but Kip pulled it back.

'We have one condition.'

'Go on.'

'Only Mzungu is to be hurt.'

'How can I guarantee that?'

'You must.'

The man stared at the money and the pendant. He downed his drink, grabbed the roll, then leant forward and took the pendant. 'Do not try to find me again.'

'What's your name?' asked Kip. He held out his hand.

'You do not need my name and I am not your friend. You only need to know I will kill this man,' he said, then left.

CHAPTER SIX

SEVERAL FURNACE-HOT DAYS
HAD BAKED THE GROUND.
EACH POTHOLE THREW THE
CART IN A NEW DIRECTION. KIP
CONSIDERED WHAT HE'D DONE,
IF IT HAD BEEN THE RIGHT THING
TO DO. HE THOUGHT HE'D BE
RELIEVED, BUT HE WAS AFRAID
OF CONSEQUENCES HE'D
NOT CONSIDERED.

CHAPTER SIX

When the warlord was dead, the village would get its children back and for him, his belongings, and his peaceful life. Tomorrow, he'd ask the villagers to help him move the wooden figure into his house.

The cart lurched heavily, throwing Kip sideways. His sweaty hands lost grip on the reins. He grabbed for the side rail, but it snapped, sending him over the edge. The donkey drew the cart a little further on, then stopped.

Kip pushed himself up into a sitting position and breathed rapidly. He'd sprained his right shoulder and gashed his left knee. The donkey glanced at him. At least it had stopped. But now he could see why: the axle had split, throwing a wheel. He could repair it, at least well enough to get home, but he would need someone else to help him lift the cart. He limped to the back of the cart and collected his tools. He dragged off a chair to use for spare parts.

Rough hair brushed against his legs. 'That's unlucky,' said a female voice behind him. More goats circled his legs. 'Or is it bad workmanship?'

Could it be her!? Kip thought. He spun round and looked down, expecting to see the little girl goat herder. Instead, a young woman stood in the road as goats jostled around her.

'This donkey always seems to find the biggest holes.'

'They seem to find trouble, don't they?'

Kip examined the woman. She did resemble the girl somewhat, perhaps it was her older sister.

'Do you need any help?' she asked.

'Yes, I do.'

Kip repaired the split hub using a chair leg as an axle rod. The goat herder stroked the donkey's head. She wore a similar dress to the girl before and it caught the light in the same way. She took Kip's bucket to fetch water for the donkey and her goats.

The goat with a collar and bell climbed onto a tree stump and faced the donkey. The goat bleated, its pink tongue shaking violently. The donkey remained stoic.

The goat herder returned and placed the bucket under the donkey's nose. It dunked its head straight in, followed by a few goats.

The girl rolled a green pod between her fingers as she approached Kip. He stopped hammering in the axle rod. 'What is that?'

'A bean creeper pod. It's meant to be lucky.'

'Aren't the seeds poisonous?'

'Don't you ever do anything dangerous?'

Kip picked up the wheel and positioned it opposite the cart. He motioned for her to hold it upright. 'Now, when I lift the cart, you must push it onto the axle.' She nodded.

Kip crouched underneath the cart, wedging his shoulders against the cart's base. He pushed upwards and when the axle aligned with the wheel's hub, he shouted, 'Now!'

The goat herder pushed on the wheel. He lowered the cart which bounced, creaked, but remained in place. Kip hammered on the hubcap. 'Thank you,' he said, climbing back up. 'We should go, the donkey needs feeding.'

'And what about you?'

CHAPTER SIX

'I'm usually too tired to cook on market days. Thanks again.'

'Goodnight, Kip.'

It was dark when they got back to the village. The donkey trotted into the barn and Kip stored the unsold items. Something caught his attention – the smell of ginger. He'd not bought any from the market, just a few vegetables. He probably had some in the kitchen, but that couldn't explain it. Approaching the house, the aroma was now mixed with the smell of stewing meat. Pork, perhaps.

He peered through the window into his living room, but it was empty. The kitchen light was on. Kip tried to remember if he'd left it on. He took the knife from his belt and gripped the front door's handle. He turned the key and pushed the door open, stepping inside. He tiptoed towards the kitchen.

The room was illuminated. A woman stood by the light switch, tall with long hair, wrapped in a red blanket. It was the carving, come alive. He gazed. 'Better close your mouth unless you're catching flies?'

She glared at the knife and put her hands on her hips. 'I think you're done, don't you?'

They sat at the dining table and ate the pork stew she'd made. It was good; better than anything he'd ever cooked. Between mouthfuls he'd steal glances at the empty plinth. He was angry with himself for not noticing it was empty.

'Looking outside will not change anything.'

'But it's impossible.'

'Do I not look real?' She threw out her arm. 'Go on, feel.'

Kip held up his hands, palms forward. 'I believe you.'

At the end of the meal, he cleared the dishes. When he returned, she was adjusting the blanket.

'I'm sorry, that blanket must be uncomfortable. It's usually on... never mind. Let me find you something else.'

'I'm tougher than I look but thank you.'

Kip still had some of his wife's clothing. He grabbed a few items and returned. 'You can sleep in our... my room. I will sleep in the rocking chair.'

She held the clothes to her chest. 'Tell me about your life, so I can place it.'

'What do you mean?'

'I remember parts of my life before this,' she said, looking down at her body. 'The conversations nearby, the wind against my bark. The birds and insects that made a home on me. The rain falling on my leaves. But I cannot place the voices I've heard to those in the village.'

Kip added logs to the fire. 'Do you have a name?'

'Trees do not have names. But now that I am something else.' She gripped the blanket. 'I shall be called Ekundu.' It meant red.

Kip beckoned her to sit. 'Let me tell you about my wife. She had a voice you would remember.'

CHAPTER SEVEN

WHEN HE WOKE, SHE WASN'T IN THE HOUSE. HE CHECKED THE BARN AND FOUND THE RED BLANKET DRAPED OVER THE DONKEY. HE RAN INTO THE VILLAGE, CHECKING ALL THE STORES BUT WITHOUT LUCK. *WHERE COULD SHE BE?* THE BELLS OF THE CHURCH RANG.

CHAPTER SEVEN

The pastor stepped in front of Kip as he launched himself towards the entrance. 'Kip, how nice to see you.' Kip peered around her, but she blocked his view. 'Do you want to come in?'

'Yes!'

The pastor stepped aside, and Kip hurtled in. He scurried down the aisle, looking across to each row. He saw Ekundu. She was sitting bolt upright in the middle of a row. Everyone around her listened intently to what she was saying, their eyes wide in disbelief. Kip scuttled towards her, bumping knees. 'Sorry,' he kept repeating. He sat himself next to her. 'I've been looking for you,' he whispered.

'I thought I'd take a walk. It's an extraordinary feeling to have legs—'

'Yes, it is,' said Kip, slapping his thighs. 'How easily we forget them. My cousin,' he said to those around him. 'Visiting. Loves telling stories.'

The pastor climbed into the pulpit. Kip waved away two youngsters peeking over the bench. He scanned the small church – it was full, the whole village must be there, he supposed.

The pastor spoke of the virtues of mercy and humility. Kip couldn't believe she could talk this way after the years of terror from the warlord. They sang hymns. Ekundu's voice was deep and powerful. 'You have a good voice,' said Kip.

'You made it.'

When the service finished, Kip guided Ekundu out of the church, leading her away from those who spoke to her earlier.

Hagos blocked their way. 'You didn't tell us you had family staying.'

Ekundu shot out her hand, 'I'm Ekundu.'

'Delighted to meet—'

'We've got to go,' said Kip. 'Must feed the donkey.'

'Another time,' said Hagos. Ekundu smiled and waved at him.

'What did you say to them?' said Kip.

Ekundu opened her arms. 'That I fell from the sky.'

'We need something more believable than that.' Kip rubbed the back of his head. 'Let's stick to you being my cousin for now.'

As they neared home, Ibrahim, a farmer, waved his wide, calloused palm at them. A coir bag slung over his shoulder was stuffed with yams. 'Kip, I need a new—' he began, before catching sight of Ekundu.

'A new what?' said Kip, who carried on walking.

'Um... yes, a plough,' he said, skipping after them. 'A new plough but if you can make me one of these too?' He eyed Ekundu from her toes upward.

Kip grabbed hold of Ibrahim's shirt. 'How do you know?!'

'Know what?'

'Never mind,' said Kip, letting go. 'I'll make you one. A plough. We must be going.'

'Nice to meet you,' said Ekundu, as she was dragged away.

Outside the house, they found the water trough lying on its side. Kip shouted towards the barn. 'I'll make you into sausages!'

Ekundu bent down and righted it. 'The trough's covered in slime, it needs to be cleaned.'

'That donkey is as stubborn as a mule and as stupid as an ass.'

'You're too hard on him. He's smarter than you think.'

Ekundu approached the barn and Kip followed. The donkey stood with its back to them, the red blanket over it. It turned as Ekundu opened the gate and swished its tail.

'Be careful,' said Kip. 'He could bolt. Or bite.'

Ekundu held her open hands towards it. It eyed her empty palm. Kip laughed. 'Unless you're holding food, he won't be interested.' Kip headed towards the house.

Ekundu began a sweet lilting hum. Kip stopped. 'That will never work.'

She continued.

The donkey's tail was still. It took a step towards her, then another. It sniffed her hands, then up one arm and finally her face. It nodded twice then rested its head on her shoulder.

'I don't believe it,' said Kip.

CHAPTER EIGHT

THE VILLAGE HAD A FRUITFUL HARVEST AND WAS ABLE TO RESTOCK SOME OF THE PROVISIONS STOLEN BY THE WARLORD. THE PASTOR THANKED GOD FOR THEIR GOOD FORTUNE. AXEL AND RUDI'S HOUSE WAS ALMOST FINISHED. THERE WAS NO NEWS OF THE WARLORD.

CHAPTER EIGHT

Kip built up his stock of larger items and began to make more money at the market. Ekundu had asked to come with him, but he'd told her the cart was too unstable with both. He felt bad about lying. He'd never lied to his wife. Except the once. Before she'd died, she'd gripped the bracelet, asking him if everything would be all right. On every journey, Kip scanned the fields for the goat herder.

Ekundu agreed to pretend she was his cousin and spent her days walking through the village or even to other villages, speaking to people about their lives and those of their ancestors. If anyone asked a difficult question, she'd laugh, telling them that some things are best left to the imagination.

After much persuasion, Kip took Ekundu to the market. She spoke to every customer like they were an old friend. He had one of his best days. Ekundu picked things up quickly. She said that, 'Even though I've never seen or done these things, I've heard them spoken of.'

Kip left her in charge to visit the tavern. The barman hadn't seen the assassin since Kip had visited. A small crowd had gathered at the stall on Kip's return. He pushed his way through, but he couldn't see her. *Has something happened to her?* Ekundu was behind the stall, balancing a chair on her feet. With a bend of her knees, she flung the chair into the air, making it spin before landing back.

Kip watched before shouting, 'What are you doing?'

The chair clattered to the floor, dispersing the gathered crowd. He held out his hand, which she grabbed and pulled herself up. They didn't speak to each other the rest of the day, yet it was his best day at the market.

On the way home, Kip spotted a few goats grazing in a nearby field. He stopped the cart.

'What are you doing?' said Ekundu. 'I don't want to stop here.'

Kip jumped off the cart. 'There's someone I want to speak to.'

Ekundu grabbed the repaired rail. 'Please, Kip, don't go.'

Kip looked into her pleading eyes. Her black pupils became swirling spirals of red. He felt dizzy and faint. 'You're right,' he said. 'Let's go home.'

Pinpricks of light pierced the black cloak of night as Ekundu and Kip sat opposite Rudi and Axel at the dining table.

'It's so lovely,' said Rudi, as she cleared the dishes.

'Kip has a way with wood,' said Ekundu.

Kip stood up and helped clear the table. 'Any news of Dayo?'

Axel and Rudi shook their heads.

'You must miss him terribly,' said Ekundu.

'We do,' said Axel, as Rudi held back tears.

'I'm sure he will be back soon,' said Kip, glancing at Axel.

As Kip and Ekundu walked back through the village, the wind caught Ekundu's dress, exposing her legs. She pulled the fabric back in. 'You never said what you thought of the dress I bought at the market.'

'It's... lovely.'

She let go of her dress, letting it whip about. Kip increased his pace. 'Let's get home, I feel a storm coming.'

As Ekundu prepared for bed, Kip checked on the donkey. 'So, bra, what do you think of her?' he said, adjusting the blanket on its back. 'Do you like her?' The donkey's tail swished.

On his return, Ekundu stood by the bedroom door in a viridian nightgown. The candle on the bedside cabinet threw ragged shadows onto the wall.

'I thought you'd already be asleep,' he said, bolting the front door as the windows rattled.

'Come to bed,' said Ekundu. 'It's not a night for anyone to be alone.'

CHAPTER NINE

THEY WERE WOKEN BY THE RATTLE OF GUNFIRE. 'STAY HERE,' SAID KIP, AS HE DRESSED THEN RAN OUTSIDE WITH HIS AXE. THE WARLORD HAD RETURNED. THE FOOD STORES HAD ALREADY BEEN EMPTIED AND SOLDIERS WERE ENTERING HOUSES, PULLING EVERYBODY OUTSIDE. OTHERS RAIDED THE GRAIN BARNS. AXEL AND RUDI SEARCHED FOR DAYO WITHIN THEIR RANKS.

CHAPTER NINE

Kip spotted Dayo in the driver's seat of Mzungu's open-top jeep, just as Axel did. Axel ran towards it and Kip reached him as several soldiers swarmed around him. Mzungu was in the back seat. Kip seethed inside; the assassin had betrayed him.

'Give me back our son,' said Axel, approaching Mzungu.

'Stay back,' said a soldier, shaking his gun at him.

'But he's my son.'

The soldier raised his gun towards Axel's head. Kip pulled Axel back. 'Take what you need but give this man back his son.'

Mzungu got out of the jeep. 'He's no longer your son. He's mine.'

At Mzungu's instruction, another soldier pulled the axe from Kip's hand. Most of the village watched the commotion.

Mzungu took off his sunglasses. He was blind in one eye. 'Our righteous war continues, but we need more soldiers and more food.'

'We don't have anything left,' implored Rudi.

'Search the houses!' shouted Mzungu. 'Take whatever you find.'

Kip launched himself at Mzungu. A soldier knocked him out before he was even close to the warlord.

The soldiers tore through the village like locusts. Anyone who tried to block them was beaten. Children hidden in chests and wardrobes cried when they were discovered.

Mzungu cleaned his sunglasses with the corner of his olive shirt then put them on. He appraised the line of new soldiers. A boy of eight wet his shorts. 'Bring the truck, they'll have to do.'

The children were loaded and rushed to peer through the wooden slats at their parents, who cried together in a huddle. Kip regained consciousness.

'Wait,' said Ekundu, 'I will go in their place.'

Mzungu looked over his shoulder. He beckoned her over. She obliged.

'She doesn't mean it,' said Kip, crawling towards her. He grabbed her wrist. 'Doesn't last night mean anything?'

She yanked her hand free. 'Let me go.'

'Can you fight?' said Mzungu. His soldiers laughed. 'Can you build a ditch or march all day?' They kept laughing.

'I can give them something worth fighting for.'

'Why shouldn't I take them *and* you?'

'If you leave them, they will be stronger and bigger. Without them, the village cannot harvest the crops you need to feed your army.'

'Let any smaller than a rifle go,' said Mzungu.

'I won't let you take her,' said Kip, standing.

'Is the carpenter master over you?'

'My destiny is not controlled by any man.'

'We'll see,' said Mzungu. 'I have a present for you, carpenter. Something to keep you company. Dayo.'

Dayo pulled a sack from the passenger footwell and brought it to the warlord.

'Dayo!' screamed Rudi, as he handed the heavy package to Mzungu. He avoided her stare. Whatever was in it had stained it dark cherry. Mzungu tipped the sack upside down.

The assassin's head fell out and rolled to a stop in front of Kip. 'You're lucky I don't burn down the whole village,' Mzungu said, dropping the sack. 'Take her away.'

A soldier gripped her arm, but when he attempted to pull Ekundu forwards she was immovable. She turned to Kip. 'When the sky bleeds, come for us all,' she whispered.

Another soldier grasped her other arm and she let them pull her away. Villagers held back the parents of the children on the truck, as it drove away, led by Mzungu's jeep.

CHAPTER TEN

WHEN KIP ENTERED THE VILLAGE TO COLLECT WATER, MOST VILLAGERS IGNORED HIM. HE NOTICED A GENERAL MALAISE. THE SOUND OF YOUNG CHILDREN PLAYING SEEMED AT ODDS WITH WHAT HAD HAPPENED.

AS THE SUN FELL BELOW THE HORIZON, KIP SAT ON THE PORCH, RESTED HIS HEAD AGAINST A BEAM AND CLOSED HIS EYES. HE TRIED NOT TO THINK ABOUT EKUNDU. SOMEONE CALLED HIS NAME.

CHAPTER TEN

Perhaps it was the goat herder.

He was shaken awake. 'Wake up.' It was Rudi. 'We didn't see you in church?'

He rubbed the back of his neck, not looking at her. 'Would I be welcome?'

'Does it matter?' Rudi sat next to him. 'Look, Kip, I understand why. Why don't you come to the church tonight? We're holding a vigil for those taken. You could pray for Ekundu.'

Kip jumped up, keeping his back to her. 'Candles and prayers will not bring them back.'

'What else can we do? We use bows to hunt rodents in bushes. We are not soldiers.'

Kip faced her, his nails digging into his palms. 'Does that mean we cannot fight?' He stood, nearly losing his balance. Rudi held out her hand to support him. 'I'm fine,' he said, shrugging her away. 'I've just not eaten.' He strode into the house.

Rudi watched the donkey chewing lazily on some straw. She turned to leave.

'Wait,' said Kip. He handed her a cup of tea then drank from a second.

Rudi sipped hers. 'Dayo loves playing football. He doesn't know it, but I watch him sometimes. He goes in goal even though he's not the tallest. He lets lots of goals in, but he doesn't seem to mind. He keeps smiling.'

Kip laid a hand on her shoulder.

Rudi handed him the cup. 'I've got to go. The elders have called a meeting to discuss how to appease the warlord.'

'The only way is to kill him.'

'Promise you won't do anything.'

Kip listened from outside the crowded tent. The futile discussions of what could be done to prevent more food or children being taken. When he turned to leave the moon was pink and a red glow covered the village.

He ran home and straight into the tool shed. He scanned the walls, wondering what he should take. Was he sure this was Ekundu's sign? Was he too late? He tied the toolbelt with his knife around his waist and left. It would have to be enough.

Kip walked steadily through the cooling air towards the warlord's fort. Within an hour, the tower was visible, black against the coral sky. Several storeys high, it rose from the centre of a wooden fort with walls too high to climb.

Kip crouched behind a clump of honey bushes, considering how he would enter. Two guards carrying rifles patrolled the perimeter in opposing circuits. One of them was Dayo. Kip tracked him, darting among the brush towards him. Something rustled nearby then nudged him hard in the back. Kip fell forward and held out his hands. He turned onto his back, feeling for the knife in his belt. A long grey face bared its large teeth.

CHAPTER TEN

'You foolish animal,' Kip hissed. 'What are you doing here?'

The donkey flicked its head up and down.

'You'll get us both shot.'

Kip flipped back onto his front and peered through the bushes. Dayo had gone past him. Kip tied the donkey to a branch and waited for Dayo to loop around. The second guard passed, briefly stopping to look at the donkey.

When Dayo approached, Kip stuck out his head. 'Dayo. It's me, Kip.'

Dayo took the rifle off his shoulder and approached. 'Who's there?' He jabbed the gun towards them. 'Come out or I will shoot you.'

The donkey neighed. Dayo fired the gun and the bullet tore into the sky. Kip jumped up, waving his hands while trying to calm the donkey. 'It's me. Kip. Don't shoot!'

'What are you doing here?'

'I'm here to rescue you.'

'You can't,' he said, lowering the gun. 'He'll destroy the whole village.'

'If he keeps taking all we have, we'll starve. Is there a way to get in?'

The other soldier came running around the front corner of the fort. Kip ducked behind the bushes and waited.

'What happened?' said the guard, his rifle readied.

'Lie,' said Kip.

'I thought I saw a... lion,' said Dayo. 'But it was just that stupid donkey. I'll get rid of it.'

'Mjinga, you wasted a bullet.' He punched Dayo on the upper arm. 'You'll be in trouble.' He slung his rifle over his shoulder and continued his patrol.

They waited until he'd gone. 'I have to go back,' said Dayo, walking away.

Kip climbed through the bushes and grabbed Dayo's baggy shirt. 'You can't. I came to rescue you all.'

'He has an army inside.'

'Then let me find Ekundu.'

Dayo pointed at the tower. 'She is in Mzungu's room at the top.' Dayo pulled away. 'I have to do my patrol, or they will hurt me.'

Kip pulled him back. 'Show me a way in first.'

They jogged to a wooden gate set into the wall. Dayo unlocked it and Kip went through it. 'Leave it open.'

The compound was a grid of single-storey wooden buildings. Spindly spotlights lit up the main paths. Kip crept from building to building, keeping to the shadows, pressing against the walls. Beneath an open window, he heard snoring and a boy crying for his mother. Torchlight flicked over his head. He stopped. A shout from inside was followed by the window being shut. Kip carried on.

Reaching the tower, he realised it was made of stone as well as timber. Two soldiers stood at its entrance. Kip circled it, but there was no other door and the lowest window too high to reach on his own. He bit his lip as he considered what to do. I can't do nothing. If I charge the soldiers, maybe I can surprise them, bring them both to the ground. If I knock them out, I won't have to kill them. Kip readied his knife and prepared to charge.

A bell rang. He must have been discovered. Or the donkey. He held his knife, gripping it as tight as he could to make the shaking stop. He closed his eyes and pressed hard against the building. It shook as boy soldiers ran through it in their clunking boots. He smelled smoke. A flaming arrow passed over his head.

Kip ran back to view the tower's entrance. It was empty. He made inside and up the single, wide, wooden spiral staircase. He climbed two steps at a time. The first two floors were open storerooms filled with food, clothing, weapons and ammunition. The next floor had a single door. He kicked it open. It was full of women. Most were jostling, vying to look out of the two open windows.

Kip entered, seeking Ekundu. He felt cold metal against his throat. 'Men aren't allowed in here, particularly those carrying a knife. Who are you?' said a voice in his ear.

'I'm looking for Ekundu.'

'She's not with us,' said a woman, stepping away from the window. Her grey, beaded hair lay across her shoulder blades.

'Where is she?'

'Why do you want *her*?'

'To rescue her.'

She laughed. 'And not us? Why should we trust you?'

A young girl tugged on her nightgown.

'He's Kip, the carpenter from my village.'

The woman studied him. 'Let him go.' The woman

behind him lowered the knife and joined the others. 'A carpenter's not much good against an army.'

Kip rubbed his neck.

'Maybe he knows who started the fires,' said the girl.

'I don't know anything about them,' said Kip. 'But you should leave while you can. The guards have gone.'

'Mzungu won't let us or anyone else leave alive. You should save yourself.'

'I want to try.'

'Upstairs,' said the grey-haired woman. 'In Mzungu's quarters.'

Kip thanked her and headed up.

The room was hazy with smoke. The walls were hung with shields, animal heads and guns. Maps were spread across a sideboard, lit by candles. A red sheet split the room in two. He pulled it aside to reveal a large, cast-iron bed. Kip felt nauseous. Did she sleep with Mzungu? Was she even still alive?

'Ekundu. Where are you? It's Kip.'

'Kip?!' said Ekundu, opening a side door. She wore a leaf-green, iridescent robe. Kip ran towards her, holding her tight to him.

'Did they hurt you?'

She pushed him away. 'Did you bring the village?'

He grabbed her hand. 'We have to leave.'

'No one's leaving,' said Mzungu, pulling aside the sheet. He held a pistol.

Ekundu stepped between them. 'Let him go.'

'He wants to kill me, can't you see?'

Kip held the knife in front of them.

Mzungu laughed, revealing his gold teeth. 'You're a carpenter who makes ordinary things that no one remembers. I am a warrior. When I die, I will be reborn a king.'

Smoke curled around them. He shook the gun at Ekundu. 'Why do you want to save this woman? When I touch her, splinters enter my skin. She's no good to any man.'

Kip ran at Mzungu, lunging at him with the knife. The gun fired as they fell into the sheet, pulling it over them. The gun slid across the wooden floor. Kip pushed himself off Mzungu who clutched at the knife embedded in his chest.

'Kip!' cried Ekundu, staring at her stomach, wet with blood.

Kip held Ekundu upright and placed his hand over hers, pressing down on the bullet wound. Her warm, dark blood seeped between their fingers. 'You'll be okay,' he said. 'When we can get outside, the donkey will carry you home.'

Ekundu stood fast. 'Leave me. Rescue the others.'

'I won't leave you.'

'No, you won't,' rasped Mzungu, lifting the gun. The red sheet was wrapped around his ankles as he shuffled towards them. His shirt was wet through with blood.

Ekundu pushed Kip away. 'Stand back!' Blood trickled down her leg, over her foot and seeped through the gaps between floorboards.

She lifted her arms towards the ceiling. Her feet grew wider, and her toes stretched outwards, pressing into the floorboards.

'What are you doing?' said Kip.

Her pupils flashed green, and her arms lengthened, her fingers stretching and growing longer. Ekundu's face flattened and widened. Thin grooves rippled down her body.

'Don't leave me.' Kip thought of his wife when her eyes closed for the last time.

Ekundu grew bigger and wider. The floorboards cracked and branches sprung from her arms and chest, forcing Kip away. Her eyelids closed and her lips fused together. The branches reached the stone walls, pushing them apart. Others snaked towards him.

'Make her stop,' said Mzungu. He fired his gun, sending wood chips off her body. Kip pressed himself against a wall and Mzungu followed him with the gun. Kip closed his eyes.

The floor beneath Mzungu collapsed. Roots flowed upwards and wrapped around his legs. He lost his balance and fired wildly until his pistol clicked empty. The room filled with branches, now dense with leaves. The maps and the sheet were on fire. Kip fled the room as Mzungu was pulled through the floor, his screams strangled.

CHAPTER ELEVEN

KIP RAN DOWN THE STAIRS. SOLDIERS PASSED HIM COMING UP, COUGHING, WITH TEARS RUNNING DOWN THEIR CHEEKS. KIP DROVE ON. THE WOMEN WERE LEAVING TOO. A SOLDIER TRIED TO STOP THEM BUT WAS PUSHED ASIDE, TUMBLING DOWNWARD. BROWN, WOODY TENDRILS TWISTED AROUND THE CENTRAL COLUMN, TWISTING DOWNWARDS.

CHAPTER ELEVEN

The tower shook, throwing everyone sideways. Kip pulled a young girl to her feet. She coughed violently. Kip tied his neckerchief around her face and guided her down the stairs.

At the entrance, a soldier brandished his gun at everyone coming out. What for, Kip didn't know. Soldiers behind him were running to the main gates. Clouds of black smoke billowed from many of the buildings. The soldier waved his gun at him. 'Who are—' but he was gone. A stone block, the size of a warthog, had crushed him.

The woman he'd spoken to before waved the women out and towards the gate. The young girl ran to her. They nodded to one another, then Kip ran for the gate. Gunshots rang out as more flaming arrows fell onto the roofs of the barracks. Kip stopped halfway across the fort and turned back. The tree had burst through the tower's wooden roof and branches had punched holes in its sides.

At the gate, he pulled at it. It was locked. He shook it, coughing violently. It rattled but wouldn't budge.

Kip got knocked to the ground. He rolled over. A boy soldier stood above him. 'You did this!' He shook his rifle, streaks of liquid running through the soot. 'Mzungu will have me killed.'

'Mzungu is dead.'

'Is that true?' said Dayo, from behind the other boy.

'It's not, it can't be.' And then the boy ran.

'It is, Dayo,' said Kip. 'Open this door so we can leave.'

'We can't,' said Dayo. 'Mzungu had the smaller gates chained from the outside. We will have to go through the main entrance.'

More shots rang out. Kip peered between the door and the frame. A soldier ran past, firing into the bush. Some of them were on fire. The donkey was still there, turning in circles, stretching the rope. The ground juddered.

'Donkey,' he whispered. 'Here, bra.'

The donkey faced him, its ears flicking. Kip waggled his fingers through the gap. The donkey tugged at his rope, setting himself free, and trotted over. It nestled its nose into Kip's hand.

'We need your help. Turn around.'

The donkey obliged.

'Now, kick the gate.'

The donkey stood firm. Kip couldn't believe the stupidity of the animal. Of all the times to be stubborn.

Soldiers ran behind. 'We must go now!' implored Dayo.

Kip checked his pockets. 'Do you have any food?'

Dayo shook his head.

Kip stuck his face into the gap. 'Remember the water trough. Kick it. I promise, I won't be angry.'

The donkey turned in a circle. Kip and Dayo stepped backwards. With a bang, the lower part of the gate shook. Two more kicks and it had broken through. Kip and Dayo tore away the lowest sections and squeezed out.

They ran through the bush, Kip pulling the donkey behind him. Bullets punctured the smoke. A dark figure dashed past him. Thorns ripped their clothes. At a clearing, Kip pulled Dayo to a stop. Kip bent over and sucked in air.

They saw a large fire and walked towards it. The elders stood around it, directing villages dressed in black. They lighted torches or arrows before running towards the fort.

The senior elder grabbed them. 'Kip. Dayo. You're safe! But where is Ekundu?'

Kip shook his head. 'She saved us all.'

The gunfire petered out as smoke poured upwards. Over half the wall was on fire and some of it had collapsed. As the soldiers fled, many dropped their guns in surrender.

Kip grabbed Dayo. 'Let's get you home.'

Dayo dropped his gun.

'Get on.' Kip helped Dayo climb onto the donkey's back.

'I remember you used to let me do this when I was a child.'

Kip pulled on the donkey's reins. 'You still are.'

CHAPTER TWELVE

DAYO JUMPED OFF THE DONKEY BEFORE THEY'D REACHED SIGHT OF THE WELL. MORE CHILDREN RETURNED, MANY WHO'D BEEN GONE FOR YEARS. EACH WAS CARED FOR, BUT NONE WOULD REMAIN UNCHANGED. IT HAD BEEN RUDI WHO'D PERSUADED THE VILLAGE TO HELP.

CHAPTER TWELVE

Life became routine again but without the fear of another visit from the warlord. The new harvest refilled their stores. The donkey wouldn't sleep without the red blanket, even when it no longer smelt of Ekundu. Kip looked for the goat herder on every trip to the market.

Kip worked on a chair outside, even as the sun beat into his back. Sweat ran down into his loose shirt as he thought of Ekundu. Their one night together and her sacrifice. To have been human for such a short time. There was a thump on the ground followed by splash. Kip found the trough on its side, the water seeping into the dry ground. But it was clean and the water fresh. 'What's got into you?' said Kip, but the donkey had left its stable.

Kip searched the village, asking anyone if they'd seen it. Dayo said he'd seen a donkey head west. The only thing in that direction was the derelict fort.

He found only burnt wood where the walls and barracks had been. The tree swayed over the piles of rubble. Some said it was even larger than the one in the village. An elder had suggested they move the village to it, but no one else agreed.

Kip clambered up over the debris to get to the tree. He found the donkey lying underneath, stretched across the roots. The sleeping donkey's chest rose and fell. 'I miss her too.'

A bell rung. Kip tried to locate it, slipping about on the loose rocks. 'It can't be.' A goat jumped up beside him, with collar and bell. It bleated. The donkey woke, climbing to its feet.

Kip stood on a root and saw the goat herder below. 'I thought I'd never see you again!'

'She was lucky to have you, you know,' she shouted.

Kip clambered down and found a woman of his age, surrounded by goats. 'She saved us. Thank you for sending her. It was you, wasn't it?'

She nodded. 'A little nudge here and there.' The donkey nuzzled his head against his chest.

'Are you a witch?'

'No!' The collared goat rubbed past her legs. 'Only out of necessity. The warlord asked me to restore his vision, but I refused. So, he killed my parents and paid a witch doctor to put a curse on me.'

'Can it be lifted?'

'I don't know. With his death, maybe so.'

Kip looked up into the dark green roof, sunlight sparkling through it like water on a silent pool. 'Would you like to see our village?'

'Will there be water for my goats?'

Kip rubbed the donkey's head. 'If someone's willing to share, there should be plenty.'

Lightning Source UK Ltd.
Milton Keynes UK
UKHW052202300822
408098UK00001B/6

* 9 7 8 1 9 1 6 0 6 4 6 5 2 *